Koni

Sherrie Begay, Kari A. B. Chew, and Steffani Cochran
Illustrated by Donna Courtney-Welch

Koni

© Copyright 2019 by White Dog Press

This book is a work of fiction. The characters and events are the products of the writer's imagination. Any resemblance to actual persons, living or dead, or actual events is coincidental and unintended. Some landscape and terrain may have been reimagined for the purposes of the narrative.

All rights reserved. No part of this book may be reproduced or utilized in any form or by any means, electronic or mechanical, including photocopying or recording, by any information or retrieval system, without permission of Chickasaw Press.

ISBN: 978-1-935684-87-9
Artwork: Donna Courtney-Welch
Concept: Sherrie Begay, Kari A.B. Chew, and Steffani Cochran

Chickasaw Press
PO Box 1548
Ada, Oklahoma 74821
chickasawpress.com

DEDICATED TO JERRY IMOTICHEY (1938-2016), WHO LOVED HIS LANGUAGE AND INSPIRED US TO WRITE CHICKASAW STORIES.

Koniat ishto

Koniat iskanno'si

Koniat lawa

Koniat iksho

Koniał nosi

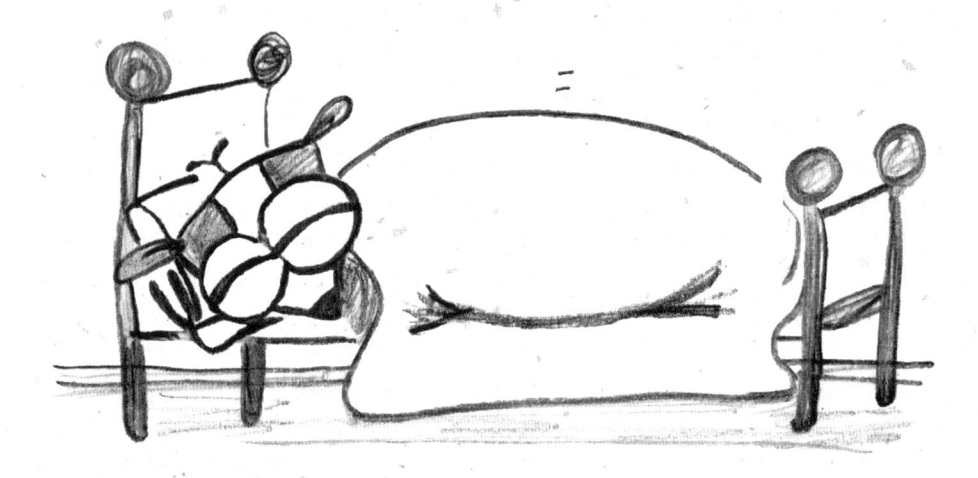

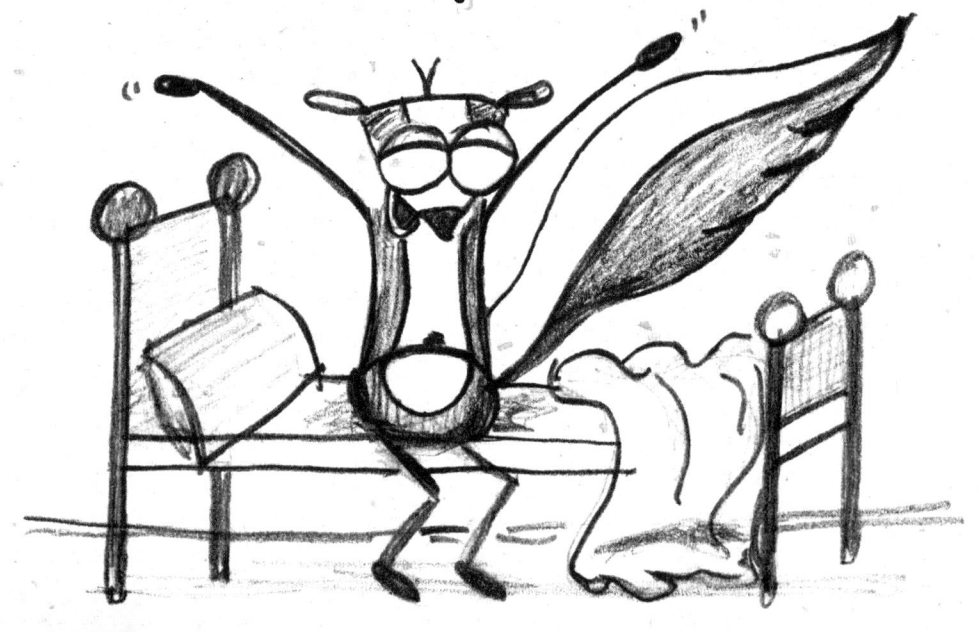

Koniał okcha

Koniat sipokni

Koniat himitta

Копият нороба

koniat kayya

Koniat litiya

Koniat chofata

Koniat Ihinko

Koniat Chonna

Koniat shila

Koniat lhayita

Koniat ayoppa

Koniat hashaa

Koniat bilama

Koniat showa

CHICKASAW LANGUAGE GLOSSARY

The Chickasaw language is an important part of our culture, and it is part of what makes us uniquely Chickasaw. *Koni* introduces our language through complete, easy-to-understand sentences, rather than through vocabulary words alone. The sentences in this story include a noun-subject and a verb. In the example below, the noun, *koni*, is the subject of the sentence and takes the subject marker *-at*. The verb, *showa*, follows the subject.

Example: Koniat showa. *(Skunk is stinky.)*

The glossary below will help you identify and pronounce the Chickasaw language seen throughout *Koni*.

Example: Koniat showa. *(Skunk is stinky.)*

The following glossary will help you identify and pronounce the Chickasaw language seen throughout *Koni*.

ayoppa (ah-yop-pah): to be happy

bilama (be-lah-mah): to smell good

chofata (choh-fah-tah): to be clean

chonna (chohn-nah): to be thin

hashaa (hah-shah): to be angry

himitta (heh-mit-tah): to be young

hopoba (hoh-poh-bah): to be hungry

iksho (ek-shoh): to not be there

ishto (ish-toh): to be big

iskanno'si (is-kun-noh-se): to be small

kayya (kaiy-yah): to be full

koni (koh-ne): skunk(s)

lawa (lah-wah): to be many of

lhayita (lhah-y-tah): to be wet

lhinko (lhen-koh): to be fat

litiya (lih-tee-yah): to be dirty

nosi (noh-se): to go to sleep

okcha (ohk-chah): to wake up

shila (she-lah): to be dry

showa (shoh-wah): to be stinky

sipokni (seh-pohk-ne): to be old

Koni

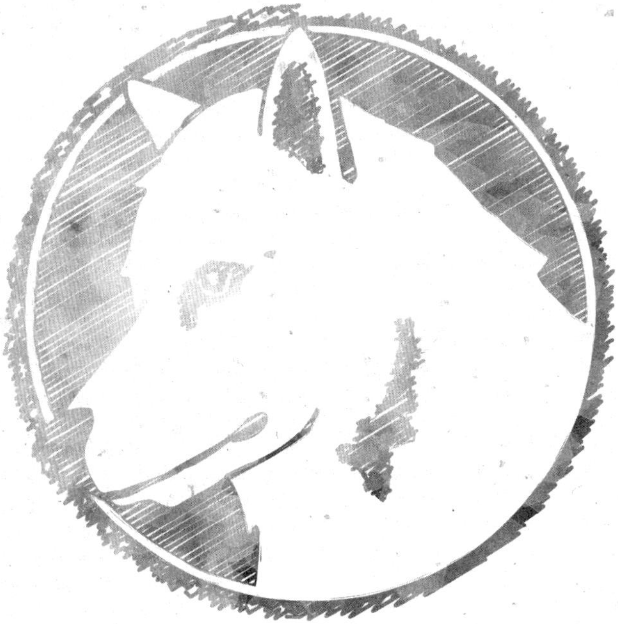